The Last of Sherlock Holmes

A Comedy in One Act

by Tim Kelly

Baker's Plays
7611 Sunset Blvd.
Los Angeles, CA 90042
bakersplays.com

STORY OF THE PLAY

Sherlock Holmes and Dr. Watson are among the most famous characters in fiction and this antic little farce-comedy pits them against their greatest foe—the treacherous Professor Moriarty. The play begins with the villain's dramatic capture. Soon after, Mrs. Hudson is announcing the presence of heavily-veiled women who have come to 221B Baker Street on "matters of the greatest delicacy." The laughs come fast and furious as the audience views a typical day in the life of the master detective, who has just discovered the science of fingerprinting. It's Watson who brings the startling news that Moriarty has escaped once more to pursue his crime and evil. Now it's up to Holmes to prove, via fingerprints, the criminal's true identity. It's a hilarious revelation that explains why Holmes was never able to outwit the foxy Professor,—with a curtain scene that'll have the audience not only surprised but laughing heartily.

CHARACTERS
(in order of speaking)

SHERLOCK HOLMES, *the famous detective.*

MRS. HUDSON, *his housekeeper.*

LADY DIMTWIDDLE-GREY, *a client.*

DR. WATSON, *Holmes' friend and flatmate.*

MYSTERY WOMAN, *another client.*
and
The infamous PROFESSOR MORIARTY.

SCENE: *The flat of* SHERLOCK HOLMES, *221B Baker Street, London.*

TIME: *The Turn of the Century.*

The Last of Sherlock Holmes

SETTING: *The flat of* SHERLOCK HOLMES, *221B Baker Street, London. Door from hallway into apartment is* D. L. *Exit into bedroom is* D. R. *There're a desk and chair* L. *A fireplace or large table is* U. R. C., *covered with books, pipes and assorted odds-and-ends, including a violin and bow.* R. *we find a bookcase and on one of the shelves a decanter and a few glasses.* D. R. *is a table with a microscope and various slides and papers. There are two comfortable chairs in the room, one a bit up from* D. L. C. *and the other a bit up from* D. R. C., *angled to face each other somewhat. There's a small rug on the floor between the chairs.* DIRECTOR'S NOTE: *The above describes the "essentials." Anything else can be added as desired.* SHERLOCK HOLMES' *digs were notorious for clutter and junk, so anything that aids in creating this atmosphere is welcome: stuffed birds, paintings, side tables, lamps, bric-a-brac and just about anything the stage crew can scavenge. Costumes ideally should be of the Victorian era, but there is no reason why modern dress can't be employed, although it should be subdued and conservative. It is late afternoon.*

AT RISE: *We discover a* FIGURE *rifling through desk drawers, frantically searching for something. The figure is obscured by an enormous cloak or coat and a hat that masks the face. We stay with the figure until:* SHERLOCK HOLMES, *pistol in hand, enters from* D. R.

HOLMES. I trust you've found what you're looking for, Professor Moriarty. (*The* FIGURE *stiffens, reaches into a pocket.*) I wouldn't reach for a weapon. It would mean I'd have to cheat the hangman of a pleasure he's long been awaiting. (*Then:*) Now, sir, you'll oblige me by moving to the door. (*Reluctantly, the* FIGURE, *his face still unseen, moves to the* D. L. *exit.*) Inspector Lestrade and his men are waiting in the hallway. Off you go. (*The* FIGURE, *head low, shuffles out of the room.* HOLMES, *continuing; calling off-*L.) He's all yours, gentlemen. Just as I promised. (*From off-*L. *come the muffled replies of a few men.* "*Thank you, Mr. Holmes." "Well done." "Come along, Moriarty," etc.* HOLMES *crosses to* C., *delighted with himself.* HOLMES, *continuing.*) Think nothing of it, gentlemen. All in a day's work. (*He pockets his revolver and crosses to the fireplace, where he takes his violin and bow from the mantel. He moves down toward* C. *and plants both feet solidly on the floor, tucks the instrument under his chin and plucks a few strings. Next, he prepares to play after a few elaborate passes with the bow. Knocking at the door.*)

MRS. HUDSON. (*Calling, off-*L.) Mr. Holmes, sir! Mr. Holmes!

HOLMES. Come in, Mrs. Hudson. (MRS. HUDSON *rushes into the room and stands* D. L. C.)

MRS. HUDSON. Oh, Mr. Holmes, what were those men from Scotland Yard doing in the house?

HOLMES. No need to fret, Mrs. Hudson. They were about their duty. You may congratulate your star boarder.

MRS. HUDSON. On what, sir?

HOLMES. I have just captured the infamous Professor Moriarty.

MRS. HUDSON. (*Name doesn't mean anything to her*) Who, sir?

HOLMES. Who? None other than the Napoleon of crime . . . organizer of half that is evil in London.

MRS. HUDSON. Was he the gentleman in the hat?

HOLMES. Call him devil, call him fiend, but never call him "gentleman."

MRS. HUDSON. I'll try to remember that, sir. (*Looks around,* HOLMES *plucks at the violin.*) Dear me, Mr. Holmes, you are untidy. (*Crossing to table* D. R., *producing a dust rag.*) I wager you've been up to one of your weird scientific experiments. (*Studying the microscope.*) I must say I don't relish all these undesirable characters you have tramping up my staircase. Scare me half to death most of them. (*Looks into microscope.*) Ugh!

HOLMES. (*Crossing to her*) Mustn't disturb anything, Mrs. Hudson.

MRS. HUDSON. (*Pointing at the microscope*) What's that horrid looking thing in there?

HOLMES. A finger—

MRS. HUDSON. A finger! (MRS. HUDSON *throws her hands over her face and screams.*) No, no, Mr. Holmes. I've had enough. Playing your violin at strange hours, revolver practice in the room, murderers and their victims in and out my front door—all this I can tolerate, but a finger under glass . . . (HOLMES *crosses to the desk and puts down violin and bow.* MRS. HUDSON *is sobbing in fear.* HOLMES *crosses to her.*)

HOLMES. There, there, Mrs. Hudson. You've misunderstood.

MRS. HUDSON. (*Pointing to the microscope*) I didn't mistake that horrible finger.

HOLMES. Not a finger, old girl, a finger*print*.

MRS. HUDSON. (*Calming down*) A fingerprint?

HOLMES. That's what you saw under the microscope.

MRS. HUDSON. Not a flesh and blood finger?

HOLMES. Of course not.

MRS. HUDSON. Well, I'm relieved to hear it. (*Then, wary:*) What's a fingerprint?

HOLMES. The impression of a fingertip on some surface.

MRS. HUDSON. Somehow, it doesn't sound Christian. Oh, I quite forgot. All this Napoleon business has addled my brains. You've a visitor waiting.

HOLMES. I suspected as much.

MRS. HUDSON. How did you know?

HOLMES. Because you just told me.

MRS. HUDSON. You are clever, Mr. Holmes.

HOLMES. Elementary.

MRS. HUDSON. You're that too, I'm sure, sir.

HOLMES. Run along, Mrs. Hudson, and show the young woman in.

MRS. HUDSON. How did you know it was a woman?

HOLMES. I detect the faint scent of rose water in the air and as you are devoted to essence of lilac, I have no choice but to deduce the caller is a young woman.

MRS. HUDSON. Not necessarily, Mr. Holmes. It could be one of them foreign gentlemen.

HOLMES. Do hurry, Mrs. Hudson. (*She scurries across the room and out into the hallway.* HOLMES *straightens his jacket and moves to the bookcase, striking a hammy pose to impress his caller. A moment passes and then a* WOMAN, *heavily veiled, sweeps in, stops.*)

LADY DIMTWIDDLE-GREY. Are we alone?

HOLMES. When Sherlock Holmes is in the room, one is always alone.

LADY DIMTWIDDLE-GREY. I am relieved to hear it.

HOLMES. (*Indicates* D. L. *chair*) Pray, seat yourself.

LADY DIMTWIDDLE-GREY. You are too kind.

HOLMES. What can I do for you?

LADY DIMTWIDDLE-GREY. I've come to you on a matter of the gravest delicacy.

HOLMES. (*Moving behind* R. C. *chair*) There is no need to conceal your facial contours behind that veil, Lady Dimtwiddle-Grey.

LADY DIMTWIDDLE-GREY. (*Startled*) How did you know?

HOLMES. I looked out the window half an hour ago and observed your carriage. I recognized your footman by the scar over the left side of his upper lip.

LADY DIMTWIDDLE-GREY. I feared to come in. You had visitors.

HOLMES. The most wanted man in Europe and important officials from Scotland Yard. The usual thing.

LADY DIMTWIDDLE-GREY. I couldn't risk being recognized.

HOLMES. I understand. Proceed.

LADY DIMTWIDDLE-GREY. (*Handing him an envelope*) This arrived in this morning's post.

HOLMES. (*Opening the envelope and producing a fruit stone*) A peach stone.

LADY DIMTWIDDLE-GREY. I thought it was plum. (HOLMES *gets a magnifying glass from the desk. He studies the stone.*)

HOLMES. Definitely peach. Judging from the moist quality of the stone I'd say it was reasonably fresh. Not more than a few days old.

Lady Dimtwiddle-Grey. Worse than I fear. The curse.

Holmes. You refer, of course, to the Dimtwiddle-Grey curse.

(*She nods.*)

Lady Dimtwiddle-Grey. My great-grandfather was the first to suffer the curse, choking his last on the pulp of a giant mango.

Holmes. Devilish things—mangos.

Lady Dimtwiddle-Grey. Then grandfather strangled to death on the pit of an alligator pear.

Holmes. I recall the case.

Lady Dimtwiddle-Grey. Then dear papa on a quantity of watermelon seeds.

Holmes. And in each case the victim received an envelope bearing either mango pulp, an alligator pear pit or seeds of the watermelon fruit.

Lady Dimtwiddle-Grey. Precisely. And this morning I received— (*Pointing to the peach stone.*) —*that*. Do you think someone is trying to tell me something?

Holmes. I should be very surprised if they weren't.

(Dr. Watson *rushes in from* D. L. *He takes off his hat and puts it down, where convenient, along with his walking stick.*)

Watson. Holmes, I just heard the news.

Holmes. No need for hysterics, old boy.

Watson. But it's shocking.

Holmes. Sensational, perhaps. I'd hardly call it shocking.

Watson. But your reputation—

Holmes. I trust that to posterity.

Watson. Good heavens, man, you've taken leave of your senses.

Holmes. Sit down. You're in a state.

(Watson *crosses to the chair* R., *sits.*)

Holmes. (*Introducing*) Lady Dimtwiddle-Grey, my associate the renowned Dr. Watson.

LADY DIMTWIDDLE-GREY. I've read some of your accounts of Mr. Holmes' derring-do. Splendid stuff.

WATSON. (*Half-rising*) Charming of you to say so, my dear.

HOLMES. I think we can dispense with the idle chatter. Watson, do sit down. This is a serious matter.

WATSON. (*Sitting again*) It will be when the newspapers get hold of it. You'll be the laughing stock of London.

LADY DIMTWIDDLE-GREY. (*Rising, terrified*) There mustn't be any publicity.

HOLMES. Pray compose yourself, Madam. You're in my invaluable hands.

LADY DIMTWIDDLE-GREY. (*Sitting*) You are too kind.

HOLMES. I surmise that the heir of your great-grandfather was your grandfather.

LADY DIMTWIDDLE-GREY. His only child, yes.

HOLMES. (*Wandering about the room in dramatic fashion*) And the heir of your grandfather was your father.

LADY DIMTWIDDLE-GREY. Why yes.

HOLMES. And the heir of your father?

LADY DIMTWIDDLE-GREY. I am—or rather, I was, his sole heir.

HOLMES. And if you should die like the others—who would inherit the Dimtwiddle-Grey fortune?

LADY DIMTWIDDLE-GREY. There isn't anyone.

WATSON. Holmes, I really think you ought to consider that business with Moriarty.

HOLMES. One epic at a time, Watson.

(LADY DIMTWIDDLE-GREY *rises and wanders* D. L.)

LADY DIMTWIDDLE-GREY. There's no one else, really. I am unmarried as you know.

WATSON. A waste.

HOLMES. Watson, please.

WATSON. Ravishing creature like this.

HOLMES. We are not discussing the lady's matrimonial prospects.

WATSON. Crying shame, if you ask me.

HOLMES. No one is asking you.

WATSON. No need to be rude.

HOLMES. I am never rude— (*Then:*) Unintentionally.

(WATSON *is offended and dissolves into a monologue of offended mumbles.*)

HOLMES. (*Continuing*) Now, Lady Dimtwiddle-Grey, to the question of heirs. No one? You're certain beyond a shadow of doubt?

LADY DIMTWIDDLE-GREY. No one that I know of. (*Then, thinking hard.*) Unless it could be *him.*

HOLMES AND WATSON. Him?

LADY DIMTWIDDLE-GREY. Great-grandfather had a brother, a scoundrel, a gambler and a rogue. Great-grandfather threw him out of the house, I understand. He vowed revenge.

WATSON. Revenge? I think we're on to something, Holmes.

HOLMES. Watson, please. It's obvious the old codger is dead and buried.

WATSON. We could investigate.

HOLMES. A waste of time.

LADY DIMTWIDDLE-GREY. Oh, it wouldn't be a waste of time, Mr. Holmes. Dr. Watson here is quite right, you know.

HOLMES. About what? Watson here is seldom right and nearly always vague.

WATSON. Give the woman a chance to answer, Holmes.

HOLMES. To humor you. (*To* LADY DIMTWIDDLE-GREY:) Would there be any point in investigating? I mean, it's unlikely the old gentleman is still with us.

LADY DIMTWIDDLE-GREY. Oh, but he is, Mr. Holmes. That's what I'm trying to tell you.

HOLMES. (*Surprised*) Alive?

LADY DIMTWIDDLE-GREY. And living in Essex. He sends me a Christmas card—

HOLMES. How often?

LADY DIMTWIDDLE-GREY. Once a year.

HOLMES. Only once a year?

WATSON. (*Cynical*) Probably in December.

LADY DIMTWIDDLE-GREY. Yes, as a matter of fact, it is in December.

HOLMES. And might I inquire as to his occupation?
LADY DIMTWIDDLE-GREY. He's an importer.
HOLMES. And what does he import?
LADY DIMTWIDDLE-GREY. Mangos, alligator pears, watermelons and peaches.
HOLMES. I should waste no time in alerting the authorities. Watson here will take care of it for you. In the meantime, I wouldn't return home for a few days and avoid peaches, if at all possible.
LADY DIMTWIDDLE-GREY. You mean . . .
HOLMES. Your great-grandfather's brother is plainly the instigator of the Dimtwiddle-Grey curse. The pieces fit, logical and exact.
LADY DIMTWIDDLE-GREY. Then I'm to be spared an agonizing death, after all.
HOLMES. I daresay you shall have a fruitful life.
WATSON. Under the circumstances, Holmes, I think that's an unfortunate choice of an adjective.
HOLMES. Quite. (*Then, moving to the door.*) Good day, Your Ladyship.
LADY DIMTWIDDLE-GREY. You're a genius, Mr. Holmes.
HOLMES. In all modesty, I must agree with you.
LADY DIMTWIDDLE-GREY. (*Exiting*) Good day, Dr. Watson.
WATSON. (*Standing*) Madam.

(HOLMES *turns to the desk and picks up his violin.*)

WATSON. (*Insistent*) What about Moriarty?
HOLMES. He's in safe hands.
WATSON. Is he? (*Then:*) Did you get a good look at him?
HOLMES. What would be the point? He's a master of disguise. Once I encountered him dressed as a flower woman outside the Drury Lane. Another time I met him when he was passing himself off as the King of Serbia.
WATSON. Clever villain.
HOLMES. And one time, in Bloomsbury, he eluded me by ambling on his knees and passing himself off as an Argentine midget.
WATSON. Fascinating.

HOLMES. I imagine Lestrade will need a surgeon's scalpel to peel away the fiend's mufti.

WATSON. Lestrade will never have the chance, I'm afraid.

HOLMES. (*Plucking the violin strings*) How do you mean?

WATSON. Holmes, do stop plucking at that violin and listen to me. Professor Moriarty has escaped.

HOLMES. (*Stunned*) Impossible.

WATSON. They were crossing Knightsgate Bridge when Moriarty flung himself out of the carriage and disappeared in among a bevy of fishmongers.

HOLMES. (*Tense*) They made no attempt to re-capture him?

WATSON. They lost him at the turn of a mackerel stall.

(HOLMES *stares in disbelief and then begins a long spiralling wail and collapses in the chair* D. L. C., *allowing the violin and bow to ease to the floor.*)

HOLMES. No, no, no. It can't be true.

WATSON. But it is.

HOLMES. Every time I think I have him, he evades me. Every time I think he is cornered, he finds a hole to escape through. Every time I plan in secret, he finds me out.

WATSON. That reminds me. How did you manage to catch him in the first place? You told me you were going out.

HOLMES. And so I did, but I returned knowing that he thought I had the plans for the underwater craft designed by Lord Brockton secreted here in the flat. I knew he couldn't pass up the opportunity—what with you at a matinee performance of Gilbert and Sullivan. (*Then, moaning.*) Oh, this is awesome. Fouled by that madman again.

(WATSON *crosses to the bookcase and pours a drink of brandy, then moves back to* HOLMES.)

WATSON. Here, take this. You look a bit washed out.

(HOLMES *takes it and drinks.* WATSON *returns the glass to the shelf.*)

HOLMES. How does he do it, this Moriarty? It's maddening. Outwitting me at every turn, anticipating my every move.

WATSON. Possibly the fellow is more alert than you, Holmes.

HOLMES. Watson, where are your manners?

WATSON. Sorry, Holmes.

HOLMES. I should think so.

WATSON. If you could only pin down his identity.

HOLMES. I've already told you, he's a master of endless camouflage.

WATSON. (*Looking to the microscope*) If you had a fingerprint . . .

HOLMES. That would be a stroke of luck. (HOLMES *jumps bolt upright to his feet.*) Watson, I do have a fingerprint.

WATSON. (*Incredulous*) No!

HOLMES. (*Hurrying to the desk*) Moriarty didn't wear gloves. (*The magnifying glass.*) He touched everything on this desk. (*A paper.*) Why, this paper is alive with prints. (HOLMES *hurries down to the microscope and busies himself with preparing a slide, some solution on the paper, etc.—all scientific and complicated.*)

WATSON. Isn't it possible you've met your match in Moriarty?

HOLMES. Nonsense.

WATSON. Give the man his due, Holmes. You know, you've always been a bit of an egotist.

HOLMES. (*Busy with his work*) Double nonsense. I'm one of the humblest men in London if I do say so myself.

WATSON. You might as well. No one else will.

HOLMES. (*Hasn't heard*) Eh?

WATSON. Nothing. I say, wasn't that Lady Dimtwiddle-Grey a rare beauty?

HOLMES. Women bore me. That's why I don't like to have them around.

WATSON. I know, but I live here, too. And I find them

most attractive with their lacy handkerchiefs and foolish hats.

HOLMES. Stop babbling. I'm trying to concentrate.

WATSON. I never have understood that fingerprint business.

HOLMES. Come here and look.

(WATSON *crosses to the table and looks into the microscope.*)

HOLMES. (*Continuing*) A new science. It will work wonders in the field of criminology. No two fingerprints are alike.

WATSON. Incredible.

HOLMES. You see the curls and the wiggly lines?

WATSON. Yes.

HOLMES. They're unique. They belong to Moriarty and no one else.

WATSON. Are you sure?

HOLMES. There can be no doubt. Here, press your thumb on a piece of paper and I'll prove it to you.

(WATSON *does. He steps back from the table and moves* c. *as* HOLMES *prepares the solution, etc. Dialogue continuing throughout.*)

HOLMES. (*Continuing*) I'll track him down yet.

WATSON. How do you feel?

HOLMES. Outraged at his escape. How else should I feel? (*Under the microscope.*) Ah, you see. I am placing the fingerprint of Moriarty beside your fingerprint.

WATSON. (*Sitting* D. L.) How are you feeling, did you say?

HOLMES. Why do you keep asking me that? (*The microscope.*) Your wiggles and Moriarty's match.

WATSON. You don't say.

HOLMES. Means nothing. We have to match the curls .nd cuts. (*Studying the prints.*) Hmmmm? (*Pause.*) That's unusual.

WATSON. What's that?

HOLMES. The wiggles and the curls are identical.

WATSON. What does that mean?

HOLMES. It means that the cuts will not match, thus proving no two sets of fingerprints are identical. (HOLMES *goes back to the microscope.*)

WATSON. Personally, I've always found much to admire in Moriarty. He enjoys life, I'm told.

HOLMES. No morals, none at all.

WATSON. A fine mathematician.

HOLMES. Anyone can do sums.

WATSON. Holmes, what would it mean if the wiggles and the curves and the cuts matched?

HOLMES. It would mean they belonged to the same person. (*Studying.*) The wiggles . . . and the curves and the . . . (*Slowly, a look of amazement on his face,* HOLMES *lifts his head from the microscope.*)

WATSON. The cuts.

HOLMES. It can't be. It's not possible.

WATSON. What can't be, what's not possible? (*Suddenly,* DR. WATSON *feels something wet inside his jacket. He reaches in and takes out a large fish—a mackerel, if possible. Annoyed, he crosses to the door and tosses it into the hallway.*)

HOLMES. (*Still in shock*) They match. That means that Professor Moriarty and Dr. Watson . . .

WATSON. (*Moving in*) Yes?

HOLMES. Are the same man.

WATSON. Elementary. (*Then:*) How are you feeling?

HOLMES. (*Dazed*) I don't feel well. (*He stumbles into chair* D. R.) I have a fever and a cramp.

WATSON. Yes, it has that effect.

HOLMES. What has?

WATSON. The poison.

HOLMES. (*Hoarsely*) Poison?

WATSON. In the brandy. Sorry, old man, but I think it's time we dissolved our partnership.

HOLMES. (*Pointing a feeble finger*) You . . . you . . . are . . .

WATSON. We are the same. Moriarty and Watson.

HOLMES. Impossible.

WATSON. Now you know how the professor knew your every move almost as soon as you did.

HOLMES. I'm burning up.

WATSON. In a moment or two it'll be all over.

HOLMES. They'll find you out.

WATSON. How? Everyone knows I am your faithful friend. Besides, I'll make out the death certificate myself.

HOLMES. Monstrous.

WATSON. Frankly, Holmes, I'm not a bit sorry to see you go. Stinking up the place with your foul-smelling tobacco. I've never met a man so conceited, so cocksure of himself and such a bore, in my entire life. I really feel I'm doing humanity a service in this. If I allowed you to continue they'd probably write books about you.

MRS. HUDSON. (*Off*-L.) Mr. Holmes, sir. A visitor.

(HOLMES *has fallen into a stupor. Quickly,* WATSON *crosses to the bookcase and gets a volume. He sticks it in* HOLMES' *hand, then sweeps the rug from the floor and throws it over* HOLMES' *lap as if it were an afghan, then a pipe which he sticks in* HOLMES' *mouth. Then he stands, calm and confident, facing the door.*)

WATSON. Show him in, Mrs. Hudson.

(MRS. HUDSON *enters, carrying the fish.*)

MRS. HUDSON. It's not a him, it's a her. Dr. Watson, do you know anything about this fish? I found it on my carpet.

WATSON. Perhaps it belongs to Inspector Lestrade.

MRS. HUDSON. What shall I do with it?

WATSON. I'd hang on to it. Might prove useful as evidence.

MRS. HUDSON. Oh, whatever am I thinking of. (*Calling off*-L.) Come in, miss.

(*In a moment, a* WOMAN, *heavily veiled, enters.* MRS. HUDSON *exits with the fish.*)

WOMAN. Are we alone?

WATSON. (*Looking at the inert body of* HOLMES) I think you could say that.

WOMAN. I've come to you on a matter of the gravest delicacy.

WATSON. (*The Casanova*) That's not surprising, considering that you yourself are undoubtedly a delicate creature.

WOMAN. You flatter me, Mr. Holmes.

WATSON. Honesty is never flattery, my pigeon. I'm not Holmes. I'm Dr. Watson, his associate.

WOMAN. I must see Mr. Holmes.

WATSON. Ssssh. (*Nods at* HOLMES.) We musn't waken him. He's had a trying day.

WOMAN. But I need his help desperately.

WATSON. He's going on a long trip. Failing health.

WOMAN. Oh, whatever will I do? I'm desperate, *desperate*.

WATSON. Shall we discuss it over a bite of dinner? I assure you, my dear, there's nothing Holmes can do for you that I can't do better. In fact, Holmes has requested that I take on all his future cases. (*She starts to protest.*) Holmes would insist, I'm sure.

WOMAN. In that case, I accept your kind invitation.

WATSON. Capital. Run along, my dear, I'll join you downstairs.

(*She exits.* WATSON *jauntily crosses for his hat and cane. He starts for the door as* HOLMES *stirs.*)

HOLMES. (*Croaking*) Curse you . . . Moriarty . . .

WATSON. Can't stay and chat with you, much as I'd like to. I'm having dinner with a lovely creature. A client.

(HOLMES *lets the book fall to the floor and slumps to one side.*)

HOLMES. (*Still disbelieving*) This can't be the end . . .

WATSON. Ah, but it is. (WATSON *exits out the door.*)

VERY FAST CURTAIN

PROPERTIES

On Stage:
    Desk with magnifying glass (L.)
    Chair (L.)
    Fireplace or large table with books, pipes, violin and
        bow (U. R. C.)
    Bookcase with decanter and glasses, volumes (R.)
    Small table with microscope, slides, paper, liquid solu-
        tion (D. R.)
    Chair (D. L. C.)
    Chair (D. R. C.)
    Rug (C.)

Brought On:
    Pistol (Holmes, from off-R.)
    Envelope containing peach stone (Lady Dimtwiddle-
        Grey, from off L.)
    Hat, cane, fish (Watson, from off L.)

COSTUME LIST

Costumes ideally should be of the Victorian Era, but there is no reason why modern dress can't be employed, although it should be subdued and conservative.

HOLMES: Smoking jacket and trousers.
MRS. HUDSON: Apron with dust rag.
LADY DIMTWIDDLE-GREY: Heavy veil.
WATSON AS PROFESSOR MORIARTY: Cloak and large hat that masks the face.
WATSON: Suit, cane and hat.
WOMAN: Heavy veil.

SOUND EFFECTS

Ad libbing of Scotland Yard men—This can be done by members of the stage crew.

OTHER TITLES AVAILABLE FROM BAKER'S PLAYS

THE BUTLER DID IT

Tim Kelly

Comedy / 5m, 5f / Interior

A Baker best seller, this comedy parodies every English mystery play ever written: but it has a decidedly American flair. Miss Maple, a dowager with a reputation for "clever" weekend parties, invites a group of detective writers to eerie Ravenswood Manor on Turkey Island where they are to impersonate their fictional characters. The hostess has arranged all sorts of amusing incidents: a mysterious voice on the radio, a menacing face at the window, a mad killer on the loose. Who is that body in the wine cellar anyway? Why do little figurines keep toppling from the mantle? Then a real murder takes place, and Miss Maple is outraged. She offers an immense reward to the "detective" who can bring the killer to justice. And what an assortment of zany would-be sleuths! When they're not busy tripping over clues, they trip over each other! Laughs collide with thrills, and the climax is a real seat-grabber as the true killer is unmasked, and almost everyone turns out to be someone else!

Can be played as a pure farce, or as humorous satire.

"...Successfully interweaves all the classic elements with an imaginative approach...a stylish cross between Ten Little Indians and The Cat and The Canary...Great fun and strictly for laughs..."
– Sun Valley (CA), Green Sheet

OTHER TITLES AVAILABLE FROM BAKER'S PLAYS

THAT'S THE SPIRIT

Tim Kelly

Murder Mystery Spoof / 5m, 7 or 8f / Interior

It's hilarious, escapist fun, a spooky puzzle and an entertaining whodunit! Psychic Jenny Davenport is murdered at a lodge that once belonged to The Great Marvel, a famed "Illusionist." Who should turn up as the investigator but another dingy psychic, Claire Voyant, who solicits the help of a bunch of weirdos: Bella Donna and her nasty ventriloquist dummy, Chester; Anne Boleyn, who has a terrible fear of axes; and Ernst Slater, the man with the x-ray eyes. Toss in some bumbling police, a fish-out-of-water niece, a crazed hermit, a walking lampshade, and a ham actor, and the results are an hysterically funny, genuinely scary one-of-a-kind lampoon.

A sure-fire audience pleaser from the popular author of The Butler Did It and The Night of the Living Beauty Pageant

"Cast and audience had a wild time . . . madcap action . . . one fun show"
– Theatre Laurel, Hollywood

"One of Kelly's best."
– Stage Directions